Don't Need Friends

CAROLYN CRIMI

illustrated by LYNN MUNSINGER

A DOUBLEDAY BOOK FOR YOUNG READERS

To my King Rat and best friend

—C.C.

A DOUBLEDAY BOOK FOR YOUNG READERS

Published by
Random House, Inc.
1540 Broadway
New York, New York 10036
Doubleday and the portrayal of an anchor with a dolphin are trademarks of
Random House, Inc.
Text copyright © 1999 by Carolyn Crimi
Illustrations copyright © 1999 by Lynn Munsinger

Library of Congress Cataloging-in-Publication Data
Crimi, Carolyn.
   Don't need friends / Carolyn Crimi ; illustrated by Lynn Munsinger.
      p.   cm.
   Summary: After his best friend moves away, Rat rudely rebuffs the efforts of the other resi-
dents of the junkyard to be friendly, until he and a grouchy old dog decide that they need each
other.
   ISBN 0-385-32643-2
   [1. Behavior—Fiction. 2. Friendship—Fiction. 3. Rats—Fiction. 4. Dogs—Fiction. 5.
Animals—Fiction.] I. Munsinger, Lynn, ill. II. Title.
PZ7.C86928Do   1999
[E]—dc21   98-29883
                                                                              CIP
                                                                               AC

The text of this book is set in 22-point Galliard.
Manufactured in the United States of America
November 1999
10 9 8 7 6 5 4 3 2 1

Rat had a best friend named Possum. Rat and Possum did everything together . . .

. . . until Possum had to move to another junkyard, leaving Rat behind.

So one fall day Rat made a decision.

"Don't need friends, don't need 'em at all," he grumbled.

"Morning, Rat," said Mouse. "How do? How do?"

"Terrible," said Rat as he scrounged for scraps. "And don't ever ask again." He grabbed a biscuit and continued on his way.

"Afternoon, friend," said Pigeon. "Care to share this poppy seed muffin with me?"

"I'm not your friend, and I don't share!" said Rat in a huff.

"Evening, Rat!" called Raccoon. "I'm having a party. Care to come?"

"Don't like parties," said Rat, "and I don't like you!"

Raccoon frowned and scurried away.

All alone, Rat slept in his crate. He could hear the chattering and cooing of the animals and birds at the party. He thought of his old friend Possum and sighed.

"Don't need friends," he mumbled as he drifted off to sleep. "Don't need 'em at all."

    Day after day, Rat kept to himself, mumbling and grumbling to no one in particular. If anyone spoke to him, he just sneered.

    Pretty soon the animals stopped inviting Rat to parties. They stopped asking him to share their meals. They even stopped saying hello.

    "Fine with me!" thought Rat. "Don't need friends, don't need 'em at all."

Then one day a dog moved in.

He was big.

He was dirty.

And he was a real grouch.

"Don't you come near me," snarled Dog as Rat made his morning rounds for scraps.

"Fine with me!" said Rat.

So Rat and Dog stayed on opposite sides of the junkyard. Rat in his crate. And Dog in his barrel. Sometimes they watched each other from across the way.

"Hey, Rat!" barked Dog. "Don't you come over here!"

"Don't you come over here, either!" shouted Rat.

At night Rat could hear Dog howling to the moon.
It wasn't a friendly sound.

Then winter came, and the nights were long
and cold.

All the other animals huddled together, telling
stories and keeping each other warm. Rat could hear
them giggling as he sat all alone in his crate.

"Hey, Dog!" Rat called. "Don't even think of coming over here!"

"Don't worry!" Dog shouted. "I won't!"

But that night, when Rat heard Dog howling at the moon, he wondered why Dog sounded so lonely.

"Forget about that," Rat mumbled to himself as he turned his back to Dog's howling. "Who cares about Dog, anyway?"

One winter morning the temperature dropped
to an all-time low. Snow covered the junk piles. Ice
glistened off old hubcaps. The animals stayed huddled
together all day, eating scraps they had saved for
such weather.

But Rat didn't mind the cold. He scampered out of his crate and called to Dog with his usual greeting. "Stay on your side, Dog!" said Rat.

Dog growled at Rat, but that was all. Rat noticed
that Dog was moving much more slowly than usual as
he marched up and down his side of the junkyard.
"Humph!" said Rat. "Lazy old mutt!"

When the moon rose that night, Rat waited for Dog's howling. But Dog was quiet.

Rat couldn't sleep. He tossed and turned. The quiet was too much for him.

"Don't start that howling again, Dog!" cried Rat.

Dog only coughed.

The next day Dog stayed in his barrel.

"Hey, Dog! Don't you move from there!" called Rat
as he gathered his breakfast.

Dog only sniffled.

"Hey, Dog! Don't try and take this pizza from me!"
said Rat as he munched on his lunch.

Dog only sneezed.

The sun set behind a mountain of junk, and still Dog did not move from his barrel.

"Fine!" shouted Rat. "Stay in there! See if I care!"

As Rat stomped off to his crate, he stumbled upon the greatest treasure he could ever have imagined. It was a foot-long salami sandwich.

"Better grab this before someone else sees it," Rat thought. He started to drag it home and then stopped. It was an awfully big sandwich. Big enough for two.

"Don't need friends, don't need 'em at all," grumbled Rat as he rolled the sandwich toward Dog's barrel.

"Hey, Dog! Don't move! Stay right where you are!"
Dog lifted his head and sniffed the air.

"Don't you dare bring that sandwich this way!" he
said, thumping his tail on the side of the barrel.

Rat pushed and pulled and dragged and rolled
that foot-long salami sandwich right to the front of
Dog's barrel.

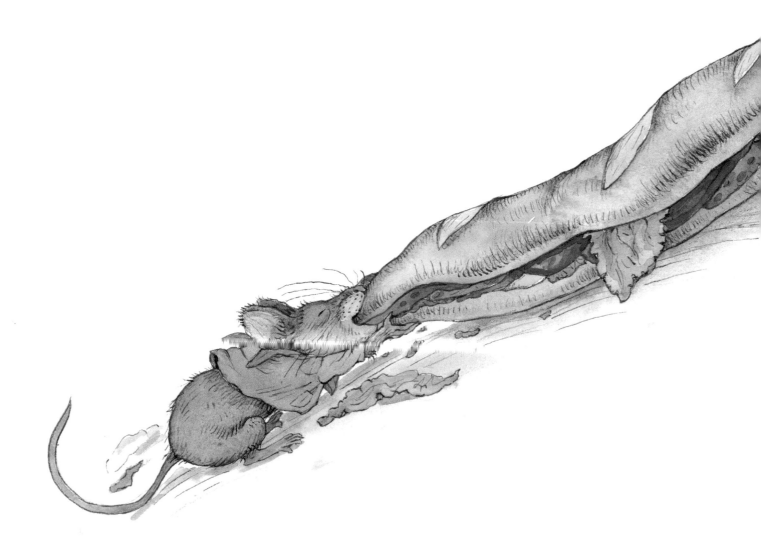

"Don't eat it all," snarled Rat. "Save some for me."
Rat ate from one side of the sandwich while Dog ate
from the other. When they were finished Dog licked
his lips and sighed. His eyes looked brighter. His ears
perked up. His tail wagged wildly.

"Don't suppose you want me to thank you,"
said Dog.

"Nope," said Rat. "I don't."

A fierce wind whipped through the junkyard, making Rat's fur stand on end. Without a word, Rat crept inside Dog's barrel and curled up next to Dog.

"Don't expect me to let you do this again," said Dog.

But the next night, when Rat came back, Dog didn't complain. And the night after that, and the night after that. Soon Dog and Rat were making their morning rounds together, searching for scraps. Sometimes they accidentally dropped a french fry or two near the smaller animals' homes.

"Hate french fries," Rat grumbled.

"Who needs 'em," said Dog.

And, when the moon was especially full and bright,
Rat and Dog howled together in harmony.

"Don't need many friends," thought Rat each night as he lay next to Dog. "Just need one."